for

M.

Library of Congress Cataloging-in-Publication Data

Ross, Christine.
    Lily and the present/Christine Ross.
    p.   cm.
    Summary: Lily searches the stores for the perfect big, bright, and
beautiful present for her new baby brother.
    ISBN 0-395-61127-X
    [1. Shopping — Fiction. 2. Gifts — Fiction. 3. Brothers and
sisters — Fiction.] I. Title.
PZ7.R719625Lj   1992   91-41134
[E] — dc20   CIP
                                  AC

Printed in China.

10   9   8   7   6   5   4   3   2   1

CHRISTINE ROSS

Lily

and

the Present

Houghton Mifflin Company
Boston 1992

Lily had a new brother. He came into the world with nothing, but that didn't last long. Within hours, presents started arriving: knitted bonnets, booties and blankets, knitted underclothes, inbetween clothes and overclothes.

"Knitting, knitting, knitting," said Lily indignantly. "Boring old clothes!"
Lily decided to buy him a real present. Something big and bright and beautiful.

So clutching her money-box,
she set off downtown.

Lily liked Biggs' Department Store. She went there sometimes with her mother. It had revolving doors that went round...

. . . and round . . .

. . . and round.

Inside, the store was very large.

"I'm looking for something big and bright and beautiful," said Lily.

"Big!" said the lady. "I've got just the thing. This crocodile is over eight feet long and once lurked in the murky, muddy Mississippi."

"It's big," Lily considered. "In fact, it's enormous. I'll take it."
It cost $25. Lily didn't have that much money. Then she
remembered what her mother always did. In a grand voice Lily said,
"Charge it, please."

The crocodile was big, but it wasn't bright and it wasn't really beautiful.

"I need something more," thought Lily.

Lily went up the escalator.
Up past handbags, haberdashery and hats to the third floor.

"I'm looking for something bright and beautiful," said Lily.

"Bright! You've come to the right place," said the man. "This chandelier has 149 light bulbs. The Queen has one of these in her dining-room. It's so bright she can read the newspaper 50 meters away."

"It's bright," said Lily. "In fact, it's brilliant. I'll take it." And in her grand voice she said, "Charge it, please."

But Lily had her doubts.
The crocodile from the murky,
muddy Mississippi was big.
The chandelier with 149 light
bulbs was bright. But they
weren't quite right.

So Lily went,
down,
down,
down,
past the hats,
haberdashery
and handbags,
then
down again
past books,
and bargains
to the basement.

"I'm looking for something beautiful," said Lily.

"Beautiful! Isn't this beautiful?" said the chef. "Lolly Gollibaggia, the film star, had a wedding cake like this when she married Mr. Universe in 1945."

"It's certainly beautiful," said Lily. "It looks delicious. I'll just take the biggest part." And in her grand voice she said, "Charge it, please."

The crocodile from the murky, muddy Mississippi was big. The chandelier with 149 light bulbs was bright. Lolly Gollibaggia's wedding cake was beautiful. Lily was satisfied.

But...

... when Lily tried to leave she couldn't get through the revolving doors!

She tried this way... and she tried that way...

She even tried this way, but she couldn't get through.

"It's no good," said Lily. "I'll just have to leave one of these parcels behind. Babies don't like cake anyway. It's bad for them."

Now Lily had two parcels left. She tried again but she still couldn't get through.

"It's no good," she said. "I'll just have to leave something else behind. Babies can't play with chandeliers. They're dangerous. They might get electrocuted."

So now Lily had one parcel left. She tried again but she still couldn't get through.

"It's no good," she said. "Babies don't like crocodiles. They're too scary."

Poor Lily. Now she had nothing except her money-box.

But then Lily saw something that looked just right. Something big, something bright and something beautiful. A big, bright, beautiful balloon! "I'll take it," said Lily, and emptied her money-box. She had exactly 50¢.

"That's 5¢ change," said the man.

Lily put the 5¢ in her money-box and took the balloon. "Perfect," she said.

And perfect it was.

SUPER
SANDCASTLE
It's the Alphabet!

It's M!

SCH[...]
[...]
130 S[...]
SCHAU[...]

W9-BCO-486

Kath[...]

Consulting Editor, D[...]

ABDO
Publishing Company

3 1257 01898 8849

READER
HENGEL, K

Published by ABDO Publishing Company, 8000 West 78th Street, Edina, Minnesota 55439. Copyright © 2010 by Abdo Consulting Group, Inc. International copyrights reserved in all countries. No part of this book may be reproduced in any form without written permission from the publisher. Super SandCastle™ is a trademark and logo of ABDO Publishing Company.

Printed in the United States.

♻ PRINTED ON RECYCLED PAPER

Editor: Liz Salzmann
Content Developer: Nancy Tuminelly
Cover and Interior Design and Production: Kelly Doudna, Mighty Media
Photo Credits: iStockphoto (Jani Bryson, Paolo Florendo), Shutterstock

Library of Congress Cataloging-in-Publication Data
Hengel, Katherine.
  It's M! / Katherine Hengel.
    p. cm. -- (It's the Alphabet!)
  ISBN 978-1-60453-600-3
  1. English language--Alphabet--Juvenile literature. 2. Alphabet books--Juvenile literature. I. Title.
  PE1155.H468 2010
  421'.1--dc22
  ⟨E⟩
                              2009021022

Super SandCastle™ books are created by a team of professional educators, reading specialists, and content developers around five essential components—phonemic awareness, phonics, vocabulary, text comprehension, and fluency—to assist young readers as they develop reading skills and strategies and increase their general knowledge. All books are written, reviewed, and leveled for guided reading, early reading intervention, and Accelerated Reader® programs for use in shared, guided, and independent reading and writing activities to support a balanced approach to literacy instruction.

About SUPER SANDCASTLE™

**Bigger Books for Emerging Readers
Grades K–4**

Created for library, classroom, and at-home use, Super SandCastle™ books support and engage young readers as they develop and build literacy skills and will increase their general knowledge about the world around them. Super SandCastle™ books are an extension of SandCastle™, the leading preK–3 imprint for emerging and beginning readers. Super SandCastle™ features a larger trim size for more reading fun.

Let Us Know
Super SandCastle™ would like to hear your stories about reading this book. What was your favorite page? Was there something hard that you needed help with? Share the ups and downs of learning to read. We want to hear from you! Send us an e-mail.

sandcastle@abdopublishing.com

Contact us for a complete list of SandCastle™, Super SandCastle™, and other nonfiction and fiction titles from ABDO Publishing Company.

www.abdopublishing.com • 8000 West 78th Street
Edina, MN 55439 • 800-800-1312 • 952-831-1632 fax

SUPER
SANDCASTLE·
It's the Alphabet!

It's M!

Kath

Consulting Editor, L

ABDO
Publishing Company

Published by ABDO Publishing Company, 8000 West 78th Street, Edina, Minnesota 55439. Copyright © 2010 by Abdo Consulting Group, Inc. International copyrights reserved in all countries. No part of this book may be reproduced in any form without written permission from the publisher. Super SandCastle™ is a trademark and logo of ABDO Publishing Company.

Printed in the United States.

♻ PRINTED ON RECYCLED PAPER

Editor: Liz Salzmann
Content Developer: Nancy Tuminelly
Cover and Interior Design and Production: Kelly Doudna, Mighty Media
Photo Credits: iStockphoto (Jani Bryson, Paolo Florendo), Shutterstock

Library of Congress Cataloging-in-Publication Data
Hengel, Katherine.
  It's M! / Katherine Hengel.
     p. cm. -- (It's the Alphabet!)
  ISBN 978-1-60453-600-3
  1. English language--Alphabet--Juvenile literature. 2. Alphabet books--Juvenile literature. I. Title.
  PE1155.H468 2010
  421'.1--dc22
  ⟨E⟩
                          2009021022

Super SandCastle™ books are created by a team of professional educators, reading specialists, and content developers around five essential components—phonemic awareness, phonics, vocabulary, text comprehension, and fluency—to assist young readers as they develop reading skills and strategies and increase their general knowledge. All books are written, reviewed, and leveled for guided reading, early reading intervention, and Accelerated Reader® programs for use in shared, guided, and independent reading and writing activities to support a balanced approach to literacy instruction.

About SUPER SANDCASTLE™

Bigger Books for Emerging Readers
Grades K–4

Created for library, classroom, and at-home use, Super SandCastle™ books support and engage young readers as they develop and build literacy skills and will increase their general knowledge about the world around them. Super SandCastle™ books are an extension of SandCastle™, the leading preK–3 imprint for emerging and beginning readers. Super SandCastle™ features a larger trim size for more reading fun.

Let Us Know
Super SandCastle™ would like to hear your stories about reading this book. What was your favorite page? Was there something hard that you needed help with? Share the ups and downs of learning to read. We want to hear from you! Send us an e-mail.

sandcastle@abdopublishing.com

Contact us for a complete list of SandCastle™, Super SandCastle™, and other nonfiction and fiction titles from ABDO Publishing Company.

www.abdopublishing.com • 8000 West 78th Street
Edina, MN 55439 • 800-800-1312 • 952-831-1632 fax

Aa Bb Cc Dd Ee
Ff Gg Hh Ii Jj Kk
Ll Mm Nn Oo Pp
Qq Rr Ss Tt Uu Vv
Ww Xx Yy Zz

The Letter

Mm

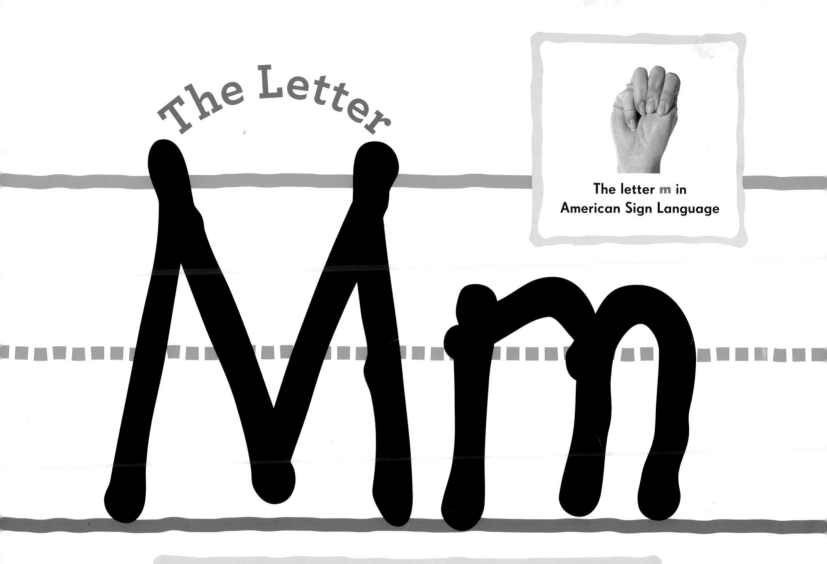

The letter m in
American Sign Language

M and m can also look like

Mm **Mm** Mm Mm Mm Mm

4

The letter **m** is a consonant.

It is the 13th letter of the alphabet.

Some words start with **m**.

meatball

mug

milk

6

mother

Matt's mother makes many messy meatballs to munch with mugs of milk.

Some words have **m** in the middle.

lamb

hamster

Samantha

Samantha plays with lambs, hamsters, and other animals almost all the time.

Some words have **m** at the end.

clam

worm

Adam

Adam had a dream that a clam and a worm chased him around his room.

Some words have a double **m**.

hum**m**ingbird

ha**mm**ock

Emma

In the summer Emma lies on her tummy in the hammock and watches hummingbirds.

Morrie the mayor has meetings all the time.

He has so many meetings, it is almost a crime!

He loves his magic markers
and images of his mother.

He watches monster movies
with Mike his moody brother.

Morrie has a major meeting
with the council members today.

But he has misplaced something
important, much to his dismay.

He searches his messy home
and his mint green motor car too.

But his favorite marker is missing,
so he is mixed up and blue.

Morrie is mad and grumpy as he mopes in his meeting room.

Without his awesome marker, he is completely full of gloom.

But before the meeting commences,
the mailman saves the day.

Morrie's mom found his magic marker,
and mailed it last Monday!

Which words have the letter **m**?

marker

milk

hamster

hippo

clam

leaf

hummingbird

cake

23

Glossary

commence (p. 20) – to begin.

completely (p. 19) – entirely or in every way.

council (p. 17) – a group of people who make decisions about a town or city.

dismay (p. 17) – a sudden loss of confidence due to fear or worry.

gloom (p. 19) – a feeling of sadness.

hammock (pp. 12, 13) – a net or cloth hung by cords at each end so that you can lie on it.

major (p. 17) – very large or important.

misplace (p. 17) – to lose something or put it in the wrong place.

moody (p. 16) – angry or unhappy without a specific reason.

mope (p. 19) – to act sad or depressed.

munch (p. 7) – to chew or snack on.

To promote letter recognition, letters are highlighted instead of glossary words in this series. The page numbers above indicate where the glossary words can be found.

More Words with **M**

Find the **m** in the beginning, middle, or end of each word.

am	ham	may	moo	pumpkin
come	jump	me	moose	ram
family	mad	meow	more	same
from	mall	miss	mouse	small
game	man	money	my	them
gum	mat	monkey	name	woman